This book belongs to
Kristen and Brandon Ward
and to the Library of
Tender Love & dayCare
From Larry & Lenore Marz

THE SUNFLOWER

WRITTEN AND ILLUSTRATED BY
MILES MacGREGOR

LANDMARK EDITIONS, INC.

P.O. Box 4469 · 1402 Kansas Avenue · Kansas City, Missouri 64127

Dedicated to:
My parents K.C. and Peter MacGregor
for their love and support.

And to David Melton,
sine qua non.

COPYRIGHT © 1994 BY MILES MacGREGOR

International Standard Book Number: 0-933849-52-4 (LIB.BDG.)

Library of Congress Cataloging-in-Publication Data
MacGregor, Miles, 1980-
    The sunflower / written and illustrated by Miles MacGregor.
    p.   cm.
    Summary: A young Indian boy dreams of a marvelous flower
and goes in search of the seeds that will bring sunlight back to the
earth and save his people from starvation.
ISBN 0-933849-52-4 (lib.bdg. : acid-free paper)
[1. Indians—Fiction.   2. Sun—Fiction.
 3. Sunflowers—Fiction.]
I. Title
PZ7.M1715Su   1994
[Fic]—dc20   94-11177
                                                CIP
                                                AC

Editorial Coordinator: Nancy R. Thatch
Creative Coordinator: David Melton

Printed in the United States of America

Landmark Editions, Inc.
P.O. Box 4469
1402 Kansas Avenue
Kansas City, Missouri 64127
(816) 241-4919

THE SUNFLOWER

Working closely with our young authors and illustrators in the preparation of their books for publication offers me opportunities to learn a lot about these students in a very short period of time.

For instance, Miles MacGregor wasn't in Kansas City for more than one hour before I learned that his favorite of favorite foods was fried bacon. When I took him and his father to the restaurant where the best bacon sandwiches in town are served, Miles and I were quickly on friendly terms.

Becoming friends with Miles was inevitable, however, for I greatly admired his illustrations in the winning book he entered in the NATIONAL WRITTEN & ILLUSTRATED BY . . . AWARDS CONTEST FOR STUDENTS. I had no doubt that he was a terrific artist, and I was eager to work with him.

As an artist, Miles has more than talent going for him. He is also very skilled. And his skills were not given to him *gratis*. He has spent hours, and days, and years in looking, observing, trying, testing, drawing, redrawing, and experimenting with pencils, pens, brushes, and paints in order to develop his skills. In fact Miles has studied drawing and painting in the same way that accountants study mathematics and physicians study anatomy, biology, and medicine — he studies *seriously*. He can draw and paint well because he has studied so well.

Some of the remarkable results of Miles's studies are featured within the pages of this beautifully illustrated book. As you turn the pages of THE SUNFLOWER, you are invited to *Ooh!* and *Aah!* as often as you wish.

— David Melton
Creative Coordinator
Landmark Editions, Inc.

There came a time long ago when the Winter People had to live in a cave on a cold, dark Earth. The warm, bright Sun that had once moved across the sky had gone down one evening and never returned. But what had happened to the Sun or where it had gone, no one knew.

Without the light of the Sun, the Winter People dwelled in a land of darkness, for each day was as dark as the night before. Only the Moon and distant stars cast a ghostly glow upon the Earth. And without the warmth of the Sun, the plants had withered and died, and most of the animals had perished, too.

The Winter People tried to survive as best they could, but they were always hungry. They spent many long hours digging for whatever dried roots they could find. Then, cold and exhausted, they would return to their cave and huddle around a small fire.

They tried to cling to the hope that the Sun would one day return and warm their land. But for now, warmth was a cave that kept out the wind, the flame of a small fire, and old worn blankets wrapped around their shivering bodies.

In the tribe of the Winter People there was a boy called Dreamer. He was called that because he always dreamed the most wonderful dreams.

The Winter People loved to hear about the boy's dreams. Each night before they went to sleep, they would urge him to tell them about his most recent one.

Since Dreamer was always eager to talk about his dreams, he would smile with pleasure. And then, he would take a deep breath and begin his story.

The Winter People would listen in fascination as the boy described places they had never seen and adventures they had never had. The grownups would smile in amazement, and the children's eyes would grow wide with wonder. And as they listened, they sometimes forgot about how cold and hungry they were — at least for a little while.

When Dreamer finished telling a story, the Winter People would roll up in their blankets, and one by one, they would drift into sleep. Then Dreamer would pull his blanket up close to his chin and fall asleep, too. Soon he would dream another one of his wonderful dreams.

One time as the Winter People slept, the Wind came close to the entrance of their cave. She sang a joyous song of a bright, warm Earth. And as she sang, Dreamer dreamt of a beautiful garden full of plants with lush, green leaves and flowers that bloomed in brilliant colors.

A bright light shone from a large yellow flower that bloomed high in a clear turquoise sky. The golden glow from its petals spread out and filled the horizon with light and warmth. Dreamer's heart was filled with happiness just from seeing such a beautiful sight.

As the boy dreamed, the Wind whispered in his ear.

"The flower you see has the power to warm all the land, so the Earth can grow food for your people," she told him. "When you awaken, climb to the top of the mountain to the east. I will meet you there and show you where you can find the seed that will grow into this life-giving flower."

When the Wind finished speaking, the flower in the boy's dreams began to glow even brighter. The light became so bright that Dreamer had to turn his eyes away from its dazzling glare.

The dream seemed so real that when Dreamer awoke, he rushed outside expecting to see the yellow flower in the sky above him. It was not there. Only the light from the Moon cast its usual eerie haze across the mountains and plains.

That didn't lessen Dreamer's excitement. He rushed back inside the cave and told his parents of his wonderful dream. But when he kept insisting that the Wind had spoken to him, his mother and father didn't know what to think. So they took their son to see the oldest and wisest man of the tribe.

The old one listened carefully to all Dreamer told him. "Do you believe there is really such a flower?" the old man finally asked.

"That is what the Wind told me," replied Dreamer.

"And do you think the Wind actually spoke to you?"

"I am sure she did," the boy said firmly.

"If you truly believe that such a flower exists," said the old man, "then you must go with the Wind. But I warn you, the journey may be dangerous, for no one can trust the Wind. She might lead you to the edge of the Earth and let you fall into endless space. Are you willing to take such a chance?"

"Yes, I am," replied the boy.

"Then go quickly," the old man told him, "because time is running out for our tribe. If we do not find a way to light and warm the Earth, the Winter People soon will be no more."

"I will leave at once," said Dreamer.

After telling his parents good-bye, Dreamer traveled eastward to the mountain. As he started to climb, moonlight spread across the rocks ahead of him. He moved carefully, trying not to slip. As he groped his way upward, sharp rocks cut his hands. His legs grew tired and his back ached. And the old man's words kept echoing in Dreamer's head: *No one can trust the Wind.*

When Dreamer finally reached the top of the mountain, he was disappointed to find that the Wind was not there to meet him. He began to doubt that she had even spoken to him and that his dream would ever come true. Then suddenly, he felt a gust of air, and the Wind appeared before him.

"Have no fear, Dreamer," she said. "As I promised, I am here to help you find the seed."

"But, why do you need me?" the boy asked suspiciously. "Why don't you use your speed and power to get the seed yourself?"

"Because it is hidden in a place where I cannot go," the Wind replied.

Then, without warning, the Wind reached down and swept Dreamer up off the mountaintop. And she carried him high up into the sky.

The Wind flew so high that Dreamer thought they soon might touch the stars. His heart beat faster and faster, and he prayed that Wind would not drop him to the Earth far below.

Eventually the gentle swaying of the Wind calmed him, and he studied her face carefully. She didn't appear to be threatening or mean. Instead, she looked peaceful and kind.

"Why do you care what happens to our tribe?" Dreamer finally asked her.

"For many years," replied the Wind, "I have enjoyed carrying the echoes of your people's laughter across the plains. Since the Sun went away, I have missed hearing their happy sounds. If the Winter People do not survive, it will sadden me, for I would be terribly lonely without them."

Dreamer wanted to believe the Wind. She seemed to be telling him the truth. He hoped she would not take him to the end of the Earth and drop him into endless space.

Dreamer didn't have long to wonder. Soon the Wind carried him to a rocky ledge and placed him before the entrance of a cave.

"The seed of the Sunflower can be found in this cave," she told him. "When the Sun went away, an old medicine woman gathered seeds of all kinds and placed them in a small bag. Then she hid the bag beneath a smooth stone in the deepest cavern."

"How do you know this?" asked Dreamer.

"Because many voices are carried on the wind," she replied, "and I hear them all."

"Then show me the way to the cavern," the boy said eagerly, "and I will follow you."

"I cannot go deep within the Earth," she told him, "for I am the Wind that moves only in the open air above the ground. You must enter the cave alone."

Dreamer shivered with fear as he peered into the dark cave. He bent down, picked up a stick, and lit it from the sparks of his fire stones.

Then he asked the Wind: "If you will not go with me, how will I find the deepest cavern?"

"Once you are inside the cave, take the passageway to the right and follow it," said the Wind. "You will know when you reach the deepest cavern. It is the one where you can see a sky full of stars above you and a sky filled with stars below you."

Dreamer was puzzled. How could there be such a thing — a sky with stars above and one with stars below? But before he could ask the Wind that question, she was gone.

Dreamer entered the cave cautiously. As he held the torch before him, its blaze cast long, flickering shadows in every direction. He stood there trembling and looked about him.

He was in the main room of the cave — a large cavern that had several passages leading off from it. And there was a damp, earthy smell in the air — a strange, unpleasant odor that the boy had never smelled before.

As Dreamer moved into the passage on the right, the odor became even stronger. Then he heard a rustling sound overhead — a restless murmur that grew louder and louder until it became the flapping of many wings. As the sounds surrounded him, he saw hundreds of red eyes were glaring at him.

Bats! There were bats swooping down from the ceiling and coming at him! He had to get away! He began to run, but his feet slipped on the damp rocks. As he fell he let go of his torch and watched in panic as it disappeared into a deep crevice. He struggled to his feet and ran blindly into the darkness.

Bat wings hit against his face, and bat claws grabbed at his hair. He was terrified! He screamed and tried to cover his head with his arms. When a bat skittered down the back of his shirt, he stumbled to the ground. But he didn't stop. He kept crawling forward until he was too exhausted to go any farther. There he lay, face down and gasping for breath.

After a while Dreamer calmed down and was relieved to find that the bats were no longer around him. But being alone in the darkness, he was still frightened, and he was very thirsty. He thought he could hear the sound of rushing water. So he crawled toward the sound. The deeper into the Earth he went, the louder the sound became until it roared and rumbled throughout the passageway. Then suddenly, it stopped, and all was quiet.

Dreamer discovered that he had come to an open shaft that went straight through to the top of the cave. When he looked up, he saw stars twinkling in the night sky above. But when he looked down, he was astonished. At the bottom of the shaft, there were also gleaming stars suspended in a sky below him.

The boy was really frightened now! He was sure the Wind had led him to the end of the Earth! And she had left him trapped in a deep cavern with no way out! Then Dreamer heard the voice of the Wind.

"Jump into the sky below," she called to him.

"I can't!" Dreamer yelled back. "If I do, I will fall into endless space!"

"No, you won't," the Wind insisted. "But if you want to find the seed of the Sunflower, you must trust me and do as I tell you. Now jump!" she commanded.

Dreamer didn't really trust the Wind, but he was so alone and afraid that he didn't know what else to do. So he shut his eyes tightly and held his breath — and then he jumped!

To his surprise Dreamer fell into the sky below with a SPLASH! He had landed in water — a dark pool that was only reflecting the starry sky above. As ripples of water surrounded him, he flailed his arms and legs, and gulped down more water than he needed to quench his thirst. Sputtering and coughing, he swam to the edge of the pool, climbed onto the rocks, and sat down.

He looked about him and discovered that he was in a large cavern. And since he had seen a sky above and a sky below, he was certain that he had come to the deepest part of the cave. But where was the bag of seeds? he wondered.

As the boy sat there cold and discouraged, he moved his hand and felt what he thought was a pebble. But when he picked it up, it wasn't a pebble at all — it was a seed! Dreamer got to his knees and began moving his hands across the floor around him. First he found one seed, and then another, and still another. Then his hand touched a large smooth stone. And beneath it, just as the Wind had told him, he found a small bag filled with seeds.

Dreamer was so excited! Surely one of these seeds would grow into the Sunflower! He looked up toward the sky and called to the Wind: "I have the seeds. But how do I get out of here?"

"I am lowering a rope," she called back. "Take hold of it, and I will pull you up."

Dreamer grabbed the rope with one hand and held on tightly. Then clasping the bag of seeds in his other hand, he went up, up, up toward the surface of the Earth.

As the Wind carried Dreamer back to his home, he was tired, but too excited to sleep. He thought of nothing except the great golden flower and how he longed to feel its warmth. At last the Wind gently placed him on the ground near the cave of the Winter People. The members of the tribe were still asleep, and Dreamer did not take the time to awaken them.

He quickly began to plant the seeds in the dry, crumbling soil. He didn't know which seed was the special one — the one that would grow into the Sunflower — so he planted all of them. And then he sat down and waited for them to grow. But nothing happened. The ground was still.

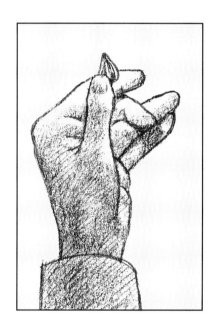

After a while Dreamer's doubts returned. Had the Wind fooled him? he wondered. Had she really tricked him after all? Is that why the seeds wouldn't grow? Maybe they would never grow! At that thought, tears welled up in Dreamer's eyes and began to roll down his cheeks. His teardrops fell onto the dry soil, and the thirsty ground drank in the moisture.

The boy's eyes were so full of tears that he didn't see the first slight movements of the soil as life stirred within one of the seeds, and a tiny green stem poked up through the Earth and sprouted shiny new leaves.

Not until the plant had grown tall enough to brush against his face did Dreamer see it. The startled boy jumped up and moved out of the way, and then he watched in delight as the plant rapidly stretched toward the sky.

"It must be the Sunflower!" exclaimed Dreamer. And his shouts of joy awakened the Winter People. They rushed out of their cave to see what was happening.

Everyone watched in amazement as the plant grew so big that soon it was as tall as a tree. Then a bud formed at the very top of the stem, and a yellow flower burst forth and began to glow. Golden rays showered the land with light. It was a wondrous sight!

"Look!" shouted Dreamer. "My dream has come true!" and he laughed and danced about.

Suddenly there was a great gust of air, and the Wind swooped down from the sky. She took hold of the stem of the great Sunflower and lifted it out of the Earth. Then she carried it far up into the sky. The higher she took it, the brighter the flower glowed, changing the sky from black to deepest blue, and then to turquoise, and turning the long, cold night into the dawn of a bright new day.

When Dreamer looked down at the ground, he saw plants were sprouting all about him, and blossoms were bursting forth in rich reds, and yellows, and purples.

The boy smiled, for he knew the Winter People would survive. From now on there would be enough food for everyone to eat. His people would enjoy the warmth of a bright and gentle Sun. They would laugh again, and the Wind would carry their joyful sounds across the plains.

From that time forward, the Sunflower bloomed in the sky every day, and the Winter People moved about freely in a land of sun-filled skies.

But to make sure his people never would have to live without the Sun, one morning Dreamer went into the fields and gathered seeds that had fallen from the Sunflower and from every other plant. He put the seeds in a small bag and hid them under a rock in a nearby cave. Then he told all the members of his tribe where they could find the seeds should they ever have need of them.

But just in case the Winter People might forget, Dreamer also told his friend — the Wind.

Chandrasekhar
age 9

Anika Thomas
age 13

Cara Reichel
age 15

Jonathan Kahn
age 9

Adam Moore
age 9

Leslie A MacKeen
age 9

Elizabeth Haidle
age 13

Amy Hagstrom
age 9

Isaac Whitlatch
age 11

Dav Pilkey
age 19

by Benjamin Kendall, age 7
State College, Pennsylvania

When Ben wears his new super-hero costume, he sees Aliens who are from outer space. His attempts to stop the pesky invaders provide loads of laughs. Colorful drawings add to the fun!

Printed Full Color
ISBN 0-933849-42-7

by Steven Shepard, age 13
Great Falls, Virginia

A gripping thriller! When a boy rows his boat to an island to retrieve a stolen knife, he faces threatening fog, treacherous currents, and a sinister lobsterman. Outstanding drawings!

Printed Full Color
ISBN 0-933849-43-5

by Travis Williams, age 16
Sardis, B.C., Canada

A chilling mystery! When a teen-age boy discovers his classmates are missing, he becomes entrapped in a web of conflicting stories, false alibis, and frightening changes. Dramatic drawings!

Printed Two Colors
ISBN 0-933849-44-3

by Dubravka Kolanović, age 18
Savannah, Georgia

Ivan enjoys a wonderful day with his grandparents, a dog, a cat, and a delightful bear that is *always* hungry. Cleverly written, brilliantly illustrated! Little kids love this book!

Printed Full Color
ISBN 0-933849-45-1

by Amy Jones, age 17
Shirley, Arkansas

A whirlwind adventure! An enchan[t] unicorn helps a young girl rescue [her] eccentric aunt from the evil Sultan Zabar. A charming story. Lovely ill[us]trations add a magical glow!

Printed Full Color
ISBN 0-933849-46-X

by Cara Reichel, age 15
Rome, Georgia

Elegant and eloquent! A young stonecutter vows to create a great statue for his impoverished village. But his fame almost stops him from fulfilling that promise.

Printed Two Colors
ISBN 0-933849-35-4

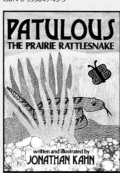

by Jonathan Kahn, age 9
Richmond Heights, Ohio

A fascinating nature story! While Patulous, a prairie rattlesnake, searches for food, he must try to avoid the claws and fangs of his own enemies.

Printed Full Color
ISBN 0-933849-36-2

by Jayna Miller, age 19
Zanesville, Ohio

The funniest Halloween ever! When Jammer the Rabbit takes all the treats, his friends get even. Their hilarious scheme includes a haunted house and mounds of chocolate.

Printed Full Color
ISBN 0-933849-37-0

by Lauren Peters, age 7
Kansas City, Missouri

The Christmas that almost wasn't! When Santa Claus takes a vacation, Mrs. Claus and the elves go on strike. Toys aren't made. Cookies aren't baked. Super illustrations.

Printed Full Color
ISBN 0-933849-25-7

by Michael Cain, age 11
Annapolis, Maryland

A glorious tale of adventure[! To] become a knight, a young man m[ust] face a beast in the forest, a sp[ell]binding witch, and a giant bird [that] guards a magic oval crystal.

Printed Full Color
ISBN 0-933849-26-5

by Heidi Salter, age 19
Berkeley, California

Spooky and wonderful! To save her vivid imagination, a young girl must confront the Great Grey Grimly himself. The narrative is filled with suspense. Vibrant illustrations.

Printed Full Color
ISBN 0-933849-21-4

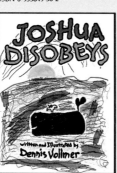

by Dennis Vollmer, age 6
Grove, Oklahoma

A baby whale's curiosity gets him into a lot of trouble. GUINNESS BOOK OF RECORDS lists Dennis as the youngest author/illustrator of a published book.

Printed Full Color
ISBN 0-933849-12-5

by Lisa Gross, age 12
Santa Fe, New Mexico

A touching story of self-esteem! A puppy is laughed at because of his unusual appearance. His search for acceptance is told with sensitivity and humor. Wonderful illustrations.

Printed Full Color
ISBN 0-933849-13-3

by Stacy Chbosky, age 14
Pittsburgh, Pennsylvania

A powerful plea for freedom! This emotion-packed story of a young slave touches an essential part of the human spirit. Made into a film by Disney Educational Productions.

Printed Full Color
ISBN 0-933849-14-1

by Amy Hagstrom, age 9
Portola, California

An exciting western! When a [boy] and an old Indian try to save a h[erd] of wild ponies, they discover a c[anyon] and see the mystical vi[sion] of the Great White Stallion.

Printed Full Color
ISBN 0-933849-15-X

Winning THE NATIONAL WRITTEN & ILLUSTRATED BY... AWARDS CONTEST was one of the most important events in my life! I'm very grateful to Landmark Editions for launching my career. The opportunities they gave me and continue to give to other young author/illustrators are invaluable.

—Dav Pilkey, author/illustrator
WORLD WAR WON
and 12 other published books

Share these wonderful books with your students and watch their imaginations soar!

As Rhonda Freese, Teacher, writes:
After I showed the Winning Books to my students, all they wante[d] to do was WRITE! WRITE! WRITE! and DRAW! DRAW! DRAW!

To motivate and inspire your students, order the Award-Winning Books today! Make sure your students experience all of these important books.

BY STUDENTS!

ILLUSTRATED BY...AWARDS FOR STUDENTS –

by Bonnie-Alise Leggat, age 8
Culpeper, Virginia

Amy J. Kendrick wants to play football, but her mother wants her to become a ballerina. Their clash of wills creates hilarious situations. Clever, delightful illustrations.

Printed Full Color
ISBN 0-933849-39-7

by Lisa Kirsten Butenhoff, age 13
Woodbury, Minnesota

The people of a Russian village face the winter without warm clothes or enough food. Then their lives are improved by a young girl's gifts. A tender story with lovely illustrations.

Printed Full Color
ISBN 0-933849-40-0

by Jennifer Brady, age 17
Columbia, Missouri

When poachers capture a pride of lions, a native boy tries to free the animals. A skillfully told story. Glowing illustrations illuminate this African adventure.

Printed Full Color
ISBN 0-933849-41-9

by Aruna Chandrasekhar, age 9
Houston, Texas

A touching and timely story! When the lives of many otters are threatened by a huge oil spill, a group of concerned people come to their rescue. Wonderful illustrations.

Printed Full Color
ISBN 0-933849-33-8

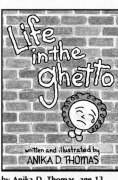

by Anika D. Thomas, age 13
Pittsburgh, Pennsylvania

A compelling autobiography! A young girl's heartrending account of growing up in a tough, inner-city neighborhood. The illustrations match the mood of this gripping story.

Printed Two Colors
ISBN 0-933849-34-6

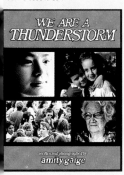

by Amity Gaige, age 16
Reading, Pennsylvania

A lyrical blend of poetry and photographs! Amity's sensitive poems offer thought-provoking ideas and amusing insights. This lovely book is one to be savored and enjoyed.

Printed Full Color
ISBN 0-933849-27-3

by Adam Moore, age 9
Broken Arrow, Oklahoma

A remarkable true story! When Adam was eight years old, he fell and ran an arrow into his head. With rare insight and humor, he tells of his ordeal and his amazing recovery.

Printed Two Colors
ISBN 0-933849-24-9

by Michael Aushenker, age 19
Ithaca, New York

Chomp! Chomp! When Arthur forgets to feed his goat, the animal eats everything in sight. A very funny story — good to the last bite. The illustrations are terrific.

Printed Full Color
ISBN 0-933849-28-1

by Leslie Ann MacKeen, age 9
Winston-Salem, North Carolina

Loaded with fun and puns! When Jeremiah T. Fitz's car stops running, several animals offer suggestions for fixing it. The results are hilarious. The illustrations are charming.

Printed Full Color
ISBN 0-933849-19-2

by Elizabeth Haidle, age 13
Beaverton, Oregon

A very touching story! The grumpiest Elfkin learns to cherish the friendship of others after he helps an injured snail and befriends an orphaned boy. Absolutely beautiful.

Printed Full Color
ISBN 0-933849-20-6

by Isaac Whitlatch, age 11
Casper, Wyoming

The true confessions of a devout vegetable hater! Isaac tells ways to avoid and dispose of the "slimy green things." His colorful illustrations provide a salad of laughter and mirth.

Printed Full Color
ISBN 0-933849-16-8

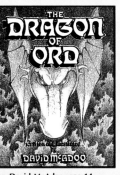

by Dav Pilkey, age 19
Cleveland, Ohio

A thought-provoking parable! Two kings halt an arms race and learn to live in peace. This outstanding book launched Dav's professional career. He now has had many books published.

Printed Full Color
ISBN 0-933849-22-2

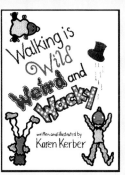

by David McAdoo, age 14
Springfield, Missouri

An exciting intergalactic adventure! In the distant future, a courageous warrior defends a kingdom from a dragon from outer space. Astounding sepia illustrations.

Printed Duotone
ISBN 0-933849-23-0

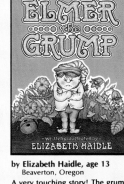

by Karen Kerber, age 12
St. Louis, Missouri

A delightfully playful book! The text is loaded with clever alliterations and gentle humor. Karen's brightly colored illustrations are composed of wiggly and waggly strokes of genius.

Printed Full Color
ISBN 0-933849-29-X

THIS SPACE
IS
RESERVED
FOR A
WONDERFUL
NEW BOOK

written &
illustrated by
ONE OF YOUR
STUDENTS

The Landmark books are so popular in our school that I had to place them on a special shelf in our library. Now that shelf is always empty.
—Jean Kern, Library Media Specialist

...These books will inspire young writers because of the quality of the works, as well as the young ages of their creators. [They] will prove worthwhile additions for promoting values discussions and encouraging creative writing. —SCHOOL LIBRARY JOURNAL

Having my book published is so exciting! It is fun to be on TV and radio talk shows. And I loved speaking in schools across the country. I enjoy meeting students and encouraging them to write and illustrate their own books.
—Karen Kerber, author/illustrator
WALKING IS WILD, WEIRD & WACKY

Jayna Miller
age 19

Lauren Peters
age 7

Michael Cain
age 11

Heidi Salter
age 19

Amity Gaige
age 16

Dennis Vollmer
age 6

Lisa Gross
age 12

Stacy Chbosky
age 14

Karen Kerber
age 12

David McAdoo
age 14

THE WINNERS OF THE 1993 NATIONAL
WRITTEN & ILLUSTRATED BY... AWARDS FOR STUDENTS®

FIRST PLACE
6-9 Age Category

FIRST PLACE
10-13 Age Category

FIRST PLACE
14-19 Age Category

Shintaro Maeda, age 8
Wichita, Kansas

Miles MacGregor, age 12
Phoenix, Arizona

Kristin Pedersen, age 18
Etobicoke, Ont., Canada

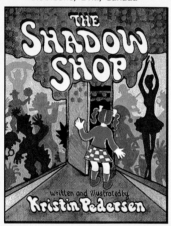

The birds will not fly in Thomas Raccoon's airshow unless Mr. Eagle approves. And everyone is afraid to talk to Mr. Eagle. So Thomas must face the big grumpy bird alone. Terrific color illustrations add exciting action to the story.

29 Pages, Full Color
ISBN 0-933849-51-6

In a dark, barren land, a young Indian boy dreams of a marvelous Sunflower that can light and warm the earth. To save his tribe from starvation, he must find the flower before it's too late. A beautifully illustrated legend.

29 Pages, Full Color
ISBN 0-933849-52-4

When Thelma McMurty trades her shadow for another one, she thinks she will live happily ever after. But an old gypsy woman knows better. Cleverly told in rhyme. The collage illustrations create a spooky, surreal atmosphere.

29 Pages, Full Color
ISBN 0-933849-53-2

BOOKS FOR STUDENTS BY STUDENTS.

Written & Illustrated by...
by David Melton

This highly acclaimed teacher's manual offers classroom-proven, step-by-step instructions in all aspects of teaching students how to write, illustrate, assemble, and bind original books. Loaded with information and positive approaches that really work. Contains lesson plans, more than 200 illustrations, and suggested adaptations for use at all grade levels – K through college.

The results are dazzling!
Children's Book Review Service, Inc.

WRITTEN & ILLUSTRATED BY... provides a current of enthusiasm, positive thinking and faith in the creative spirit of children. David Melton has the heart of a teacher.
THE READING TEACHER

...an exceptional book! Just browsing through it stimulates excitement for writing
Joyce E. Juntune, Executive Director
The National Association for Creativity

A "how to" book that really works.
Judy O'Brien, Teacher

Softcover, 96 Pages
ISBN 0-933849-00-1

LANDMARK EDITIONS, INC.
P.O. BOX 4469 • KANSAS CITY, MISSOURI 64127 • (816) 241-4919